Equal Access
Fighting for Disability Protections™

Beating Bullying Against Teens with Disabilities

Lisa A. Crayton

Rosen
YA™
New York

To my family, who taught me how to embrace and celebrate my physical difference and joyfully reach for my goals without limitation

Published in 2020 by The Rosen Publishing Group, Inc.
29 East 21st Street, New York, NY 10010

First Edition

Library of Congress Cataloging-in-Publication Data

Names: Crayton, Lisa A., author.
Title: Beating bullying against teens with disabilities / Lisa A. Crayton.
Description: First edition. | New York, NY : Rosen Publishing, 2020. | Series: Equal access: fighting for disability protections | Includes bibliographical references and index.
Identifiers: LCCN 2018011825| ISBN 9781508183341 (library bound) | ISBN 9781508183334 (pbk.)
Subjects: LCSH: Bullying—Prevention—Juvenile literature. | Teenagers with disabilities—Juvenile literature. | Interpersonal conflict in adolescence—Juvenile literature. | Self-esteem in adolescence—Juvenile literature.
Classification: LCC BF637.B85 C73 2019 | DDC 302.34/3087—dc23
LC record available at https://lccn.loc.gov/2018011825

Manufactured in the United States of America

The editors of this resource have consulted various organizations' style guides, including that of the National Center on Disability and Journalism, to ensure the language herein is accurate, sensitive, and respectful. In accordance with NCDJ's recommendation, we have deferred to our author's preference of either people-first or identity-first language.

For some of the images in this book, the people photographed are models and the depictions do not imply actual situations or events.

Contents

Introduction

Bullying makes teens sick—literally. Sleepless nights. Stomach pain and nausea. Headaches. Depression. Anxiety attacks. All of these are effects of bullying, a social issue affecting more than three million students a year.

Bullying affects teens of all ages and genders. In addition, according to the Stopbullying.gov website (https://www.stopbullying.gov), a division of the US Department of Health and Human Services, 70.6 percent of students have witnessed bullying at school. This frequency is no surprise to teens with disabilities, who often have to deal with this problem on a daily basis.

Bullies pick on teens who seem vulnerable, particularly those who have few friends or are introverts or appear to have issues with confidence or self-esteem. And bullies go after students who are considered different, including those with physical, learning, and developmental disabilities.

Once seen as a normal part of growing up, bullying is recognized today as a widespread, harmful social problem. According to StopBullying.gov, in 2011, 28 percent of US students in sixth through twelfth grades were bullied. In 2015, 20 percent of US students in ninth to twelfth grades were bullied.

The alarming frequency of bullying is even higher for teens with disabilities. According to Stopbullying.gov having a "special health need" puts a student at a higher risk of bullying than their peers.

Teens with disabilities who are bullied at school, home, or in the community may develop stress-related symptoms such as headaches, stomachaches, and anxiety.

It cites epilepsy or a food allergy as examples. But teens with other disabilities are also affected. Bullying victims include teens with physical disabilities, such as those who are missing limbs from birth, those with dwarfism, or those with visual impairments. Teens with dyslexia and other learning disabilities, autism and other developmental disabilities, and Tourette's syndrome and other disorders affecting the nervous system are also affected.

Bullied teens need to know that they are not to blame for the way they are treated. Some teens with disabilities bully their peers. In some of these cases, the bully may have been a victim and is striking back. Teens with disabilities who bully should seek help to address underlying causes and discover ways to stop their destructive behavior.

If you are being bullied, learning strategies for beating bullying helps you address the issue. The most effective cure for bullying is concentrated doses of awareness and resistance. Teens with disabilities can beat bullying by staunchly, and safely, confronting it wherever it happens.

Chapter One

Bullying Up Close

Teens with disabilities may look, act, speak, or mentally or emotionally process things differently from other teens. Some may have limited or no use of one or more senses, such as hearing. Others use equipment such as a wheelchair or a cane that further differentiates them from peers. Those truths can't be denied.

But a greater truth makes them some of the world's unsung, real-life heroes. Collectively, they are daily examples of courage and grit as they overcome challenges at home, at school, and in their communities. Despite this, many teens with disabilities are victims of bullying.

A Common Problem

According to the PACER's National Bullying Prevention Center (https://www.pacer.org/bullying) more than 60 percent of teens with disabilities report being bullied. According to PACER, the rate of bullying among teens with disabilities varies based on the disability. It notes the following rates for students with certain disabilities: behavioral and emotional disorders (35.3 percent), intellectual disabilities (20.8 percent), autism (24.3 percent), health impairments (20.8 percent), and other specific learning disabilities (19 percent).

Like all students, teens with disabilities want to feed their hunger for knowledge. They want to make and keep friends and have fun during school while being engaged in learning. They also seek acceptance and want others to recognize that a disability does not fully define who they are and what they are capable of doing. What they do not want is to be picked on because of a perceived or actual limitation. Yet many are still bullied.

It's difficult for bullied teens to pay attention to the teacher or participate in class discussions when they are worried about what type of bullying behavior they'll have to deal with next.

Bullying is using words or actions to threaten or harm a teen with a disability. The Centers for Disease Control and Prevention (CDC) and the Department of Education (DOE) developed a set of federal definitions for bullying in 2014. They define bullying as either direct or indirect and place it in four categories: physical, verbal, relational, and damage to property.

If the behavior hurts, it's bullying. If it belittles, making you feel inferior because of a condition, it's bullying. If it scares, depresses, or makes you feel like harming yourself, it is bullying.

Sometimes bullying is very obvious, like a slap on the back of the head of a teen seated in a wheelchair. Other times, it's subtler. Perhaps the bully blocks an entryway to a classroom so the student in a wheelchair can't easily maneuver through the door. Bullying that falls into the second category may make a teen wonder, "Was that deliberate?"

Bullying in its strictest sense is repeated behavior. Frequency is a key to determining if someone's actions are accidental or purposeful.

Some bullying is obvious, such as blocking a door so that a student who uses a wheelchair can't make his way through the entryway.

Analyzing Actions

Bullying varies in its type and severity. Physical bullying includes harmful touching, pinching, kicking, hitting, hair pulling, and more. Some physical bullying may violate the Americans with Disabilities Act (ADA). The ADA protects teens against discrimination based on a disability. It is a civil rights law offering expanded protections than those originally covered under the Individuals with Disabilities Education Act (IDEA), which was enacted in 1975. IDEA assures safe learning environments that foster education without restrictions. Under the IDEA, a teen with a disability could get help beating bullying by exercising his right to a safe academic environment.

In addition to physical bullying, there are other types of bullying. Examples include psychological, social, and verbal bullying as well as hazing and cyberbullying.

Regardless of its type, bullying is never acceptable. Teens with disabilities are not doormats for bullies to wipe their aggression on. They do not have to endure such treatment. Safely addressing all incidences of bullying helps teens escape from the related fear, frustration, and harm.

Who Is Bullied

Disabilities occur for various reasons. Some may be linked to a condition a teen has had since birth, such as Down syndrome, or an illness such as type 1 diabetes that occurs at a young age. Other

✋ ADA: Civil Rights Protection

For almost thirty years, the Americans with Disabilities Act (ADA) has protected the civil rights of people with disabilities. The ADA states that its purpose is "to provide a clear and comprehensive mandate for the elimination of discrimination against individuals with disabilities."

The ADA is designed to give people with mental and physical impairments the same access to opportunities as everyone else. It is designed to include far-reaching protections, including schools, workplaces, housing, transportation, and public accommodations, under its umbrella.

A bully who targets a teen amputee, for example, because of that condition is violating the ADA. It is disability-targeted bullying and illegal.

disabilities stem from something that happenned later on in life, such as a sports injury, car accident, abuse, or other trauma. To be defined as a disability, the condition must cause some kind of physical, mental, emotional, or other limitation, including chronic pain.

Bullies don't care what type of disability affects a teen, whether she can defend herself, or even understands what bullying is.

11

Bullies may view teens with disabilities as being more vulnerable than other peers. A bully will even heap abuse on a teen who doesn't fully understand that he is the target of bullying.

Bullies target teens with all types of conditions, including those that affect a student's:

Body: including physical disabilities such as missing limbs, paraplegia, dwarfism; and chronic illness such as diabetes or severe allergies

Mind and emotions: including autism and other developmental disabilities; learning disabilities, such as attention-deficit hyperactivity disorder (ADHD), obsessive-compulsive disorder (OCD), and bipolar disorder

Nervous system: including cerebral palsy and Tourette's syndrome

Senses: including low vision, hearing loss, or an inability to speak

Who Bullies

There is no one portrait of a bully. Bullies represent all walks of life. They are male and female. They are black, white, Hispanic, and other races. Some might be familiar to teens with disabilities while others are strangers. Teens often think bullies are kids from poor backgrounds, loners, or those who are underachievers at school. However, popular students, athletes, and students with high GPAs are also bullies.

Bullies seek power and control and will do anything they can to be in charge. Bullies act aggressively to make teens with disabilities feel afraid of them. They believe fearful teens won't try to stop the abuse or report it to a trusted adult and will just give them whatever they want.

Many bullies pretend to be powerful but struggle with feelings of inferiority. Perhaps they are embarrassed by their poor academic performance or feel unattractive. They attempt to cover up their inferiority complex by hurting teens with disabilities. They may also feel pressured to bully. To be accepted among their cliques, they either initiate acts, join in with their friends, or do not report bullying they witness.

Mean girls specialize in fear tactics. Like some other bullies, they act out because they feel inferior. They sometimes believe they are not pretty, athletically gifted, or smart so they bully teens who are. They also act petty, excluding girls with disabilities from social gatherings, conversations, or other social interactions.

13

Sadly, sometimes a bully is the very person who was once a victim. That person tries to recover a perceived loss of power by preying on other teens. It's a vicious cycle that never closes because bullying doesn't make a person feel better, only worse!

There is another, more troubling and emotionally devastating, type of bullying. It occurs when a friend betrays another friend and bullies, either alone or with a clique. That bully may engage in such verbal or physical abuse as:

- Ridiculing a teen in front of other people
- Excluding a teen from some or all activities to which he or she once freely participated, such as eating lunch together or being invited to sleepovers or afterschool outings
- Making fun of a teen's clothing, possessions, body (weight, odor, height), or skills (such as playing an instrument or sports)
- Sharing a former friend's secrets
- Mocking a teen's disability

True friends would never, ever do any of those things.

Regardless of the cause, bullying hurts. It causes short- and long-term problems for victims. Sometimes the effects last for years. If you're struggling to overcome bullying, seek help from parents or other trusted adults.

Myths & Facts

Myth: If a teen did not have a disability she would not be bullied.

Fact: Many teens are bullied, not just those with disabilities.

Myth: Teasing is harmless, and not bullying.

Fact: Continual teasing can be a form of bullying, and it's never okay to tease anyone about a disability.

Myth: If a teen has a disability he will not bully another teen with a disability.

Fact: As difficult as it is to understand, sometimes teens with disabilities bully their peers.

Chapter Two

No Place to Hide

Bullying happens everywhere. Teens with disabilities may encounter it at home, in a movie theater, at a park, in a classroom, and any other places they regularly go. Because it is so pervasive, bullying can seem overwhelming. It also may seem unbeatable. Yet beating bullying is possible. After you begin to understand what bullying is, who is bullied, and who bullies, you can better understand where bullying occurs, the effects of bullying, and how to respond to attacks.

Hurt at Home

Bullying can first take place at home. A girl may hit, tease, or coerce her brother to do what she wants without repercussions. A boy may see a parent bully another relative and think that it is okay to act that way. Teens may be bullied by visitors who come to their homes. That person could be a cousin or relative, a neighbor, or even a friend.

Perhaps some of the most shocking incidences come from an unexpected source: adults. Adults may act aggressively, intimidate a teen, ridicule, or physically hurt her. That adult could be a relative, friend of a parent, medical professional who provides in-home care for a family member, or some other adult.

Home is supposed to be a safe haven for kids. Bullying changes that. When bullying happens at home or the perpetrator is a family member or friend, students can feel confused, betrayed, or angry. Some may become withdrawn and unfriendly. Others might strike back by bullying people in their orbit.

A sad fact about bullying is that it can occur at home, turning what should be a safe haven into a place that makes a teen with a disability feel fearful, anxious, and alone.

School Blues

Schools are supposed to offer safe learning environments, but many kids with disabilities are first confronted by bullies in a school setting.

According to Dosomething.org (https://www .dosomething.org/us), an organization that encourages activism, more than 70 percent of students

Naomi Hirabayashi, CMO of DoSomething, an organization that encourages young people to take part in activism, speaks at a 2015 antibullying event in New York City.

state that bullying is a problem at school. Repeated bullying is the reason why 10 percent of students who drop out of school do so.

At school, some of the places where bullying happens include:

- Classrooms, where teens are mocked while answering questions or ostracized while working on group projects
- Bathrooms, where teens with disabilities are blocked from using handicapped stalls or physically attacked
- Lunchrooms, where bullies block access to tables or chairs, tamper with a teen's food, or knock trays over
- Hallways, where teens are called names, pushed around, or have their possessions grabbed and tossed from one bully to another
- Gymnasiums, where bullies hit, push, or otherwise physically harm teens with disabilities while pretending they were sports-related accidents
- Auditoriums, where teens are booed while

performing or mocked and taunted while seated next to bullies

- School buses, where teens are physically or verbally assaulted or barred from getting out of their seats when their stop approaches

Community Concerns

Throughout the community, there are places where teens with disabilities risk being bullied. Bullies could sit behind a victim at a movie theater, pushing her seat with their feet or throwing popcorn. Bullying can also happen at local parks, stores, or anywhere else people gather.

Many teens hang out in fast-food restaurants, where teens with disabilities can encounter aggressive behavior from their peers, restaurant staff, or other patrons. Bullies can taunt or tease their victims or make their victims buy them food. Teens who work at fast-food places may face bullying from other teen workers, supervisors, or customers. For example, a teen with a learning disability may be ridiculed by staff or patrons for taking more time to take or ring up orders.

Devastating Effects

Bullying takes a toll on a teen with disabilities. It can spark repeated absenteeism, as well as cause bullied teens to drop out of school. Teens who are bullied may develop stress-related ailments, such

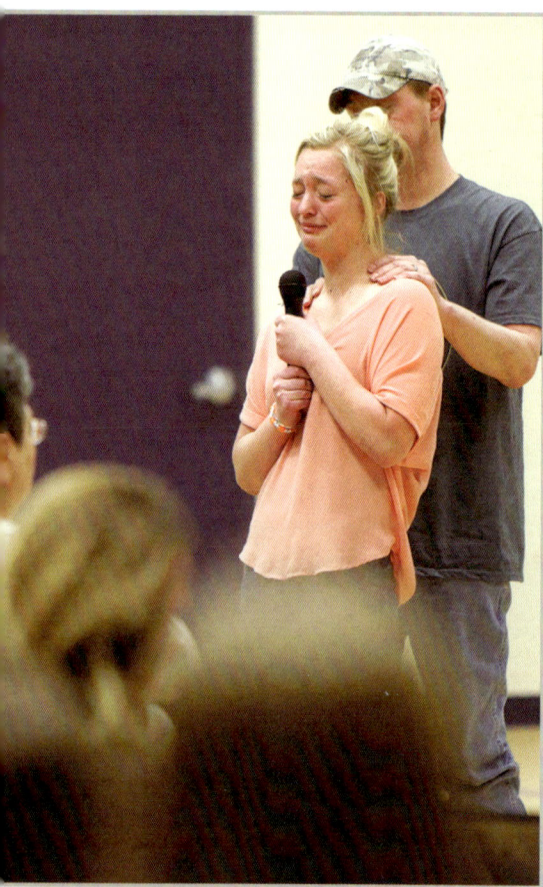

In this photo Katlyn Gillen discusses the suicide of her brother Deon, who had learning disabilities and was bullied by classmates at Park High School in Livingston, Montana.

as headaches and stomachaches. Bullied teens can also sustain injuries when they are physically abused, which require immediate care.

Some teens experience depression or other mental health problems as a result of bullying. When teens with disabilities can no longer cope with the abuse, some resort to bullycide, which is bullying-related suicide.

Bullying also affects bullies and bystanders. Bystanders are other students who may witness or be aware of troublesome incidents. Bullies experience increased risk of substance abuse. Bystanders suffer from many of the same negative effects as victims when they witness an attack.

Warning Signs

There are warning signs that suggest someone is being bullied. He or she may get headaches a lot,

✋ A Pledge Worth Making

How do you get students to stop bullying one another? Schools throughout the nation have had their students sign antibullying pledges to help reduce incidences of bullying.

At the heart of the pledges is a commitment to antibullying principles that teens are encouraged to follow. The pledges remind teens to be accepting of all of their peers, no matter their differences, disabilities, or gender identifications.

If teens with disabilities attend a school where pledges have already been implemented, they can sign up to become antibullying advocates alongside their peers. If there is no antibullying program at their school, they can speak with teachers, guidance counselors, or other school personnel to learn how to develop this type of program.

stop eating at school, and have injuries that seem to appear for no apparent reason.

Being aggressive and acting mean with friends or relatives can be a sign someone is being bullied but not being open about it. Bullying other teens is also a sign, as some victims retaliate by hurting other students. Self-harm is another warning

✋ Five Signs of a Bully

What makes a student at risk of becoming a bully?

- She hangs out with mean girls or other bullies.
- She plays the blame game, citing others for her issues.
- He is a constant fighter.
- Her aggression is off the charts.
- His second classroom is detention or the principal's office.

Why are those warning signs important? Because bullying is a global issue and in our increasingly connected world, teens do not have to leave home to make contact with bullies abroad. Instead they can be victims of cyberbullying, which occurs through the use of electronic devices. Indeed, teens can encounter bullies on social media, in chat rooms, and on games that have internet connections that allow teens to play with or against teens in other cities, states, or countries.

sign. If hurting yourself starts to seem like a way to stop the bullying, get help before things escalate. It's not the solution to your problem. Reach out to a friend for help. Talk to a parent or other trusted adult. Call the National Suicide Prevention Lifeline (800-273-8255) to have a confidential talk about bullying and its impact on you. If a friend starts hurting himself, reach out to him or a trusted adult. He may be at risk for worse injuries or even suicide.

How to Respond to Bullying

It may seem like there is no place that is bully proof. There is some truth to that. Teens with disabilities, however, can learn to respond effectively.

Responding to bullying takes courage. It also takes a safety-first attitude. At no time should a

Students help prevent more than half of all bullying incidents when they intervene to stop peers from attacking a potential victim.

teen try to address bullying if it could cause further harm to himself.

The key is to respond in ways that stop bullying without causing harm. Any other approach, such as retaliation, results in consequences at school and elsewhere. Teens can't expect to overcome bullying by becoming troublemakers themselves.

Knowing the warning signs of bullying is a first step in beating bullying. It provides teens with disabilities a way to detect, and possibly avoid, danger. Getting help from peers also is beneficial. According to PACER's National Bullying Center, 57 percent of incidences of bullying are stopped when another student intervenes on behalf of a bullied teen. Teachers, guidance counselors, and other trusted adults can also be good resources if you're looking for help combating bullying. As a result of changing attitudes, today's teens with disabilities are living at a time when help for bullying is greater than ever. There is no need to feel alone.

Chapter Three

How It Happens

Bullies are cunning. They take advantage of moments when intended victims are alone or with other teens who are unlikely to stop an attack. These opportunists also are adept at doing their dirty work when no adult is around.

In a typical day, teens with disabilities could face cruel behavior at any time. Before the first bell, a bully might corner a teen with Crohn's disease in a bathroom and shove him against a wall, bar his exit from a stall, or demand a cellphone or other possession. No one is the wiser because the bully then walks out the door as if nothing has happened.

Bathrooms are just one of the places around school where bullying occurs. And the timing of a bully's troubling actions also varies. In a locker room before an early afternoon gym class, girls might surround a female teen who has been diagnosed with bipolar disorder and began calling her names that demean her condition, such as crazy or nutjob.

In an after-school tutoring session, a teen with dwarfism could have difficulty focusing on the tutor or materials if a group of bullies strategically sits in front of him, twisting in their seats and otherwise purposefully blocking his view.

Intimidation is a form of bullying. Taunts, ridicule, and threats can make a teen with a disability feel so overwhelmed that she can barely cope.

At three different times a day, these are three ways bullies could pester students to make their school days miserable. Bullies really are that relentless.

The following news reports illustrate some tactics bullies use to target their victims:

In Crystal, Minnesota, a boy with a physical disability was attacked in a store by a group of teens on September 18, 2017. They then posted the video of the attack on Facebook.

In Nashville, Tennessee, a teen's wig was ripped off by a bully on January 28, 2018. The girl did not care that the victim wore the wig because of a scalp condition. The victim suffered whiplash and abrasions in the attack. The perpetrator then resorted to cyberbullying. She took a video of her victim in the bathroom crying after the painful, humiliating incident and shared it on the social media app Snapchat.

A teen with a heart condition in Gisborne, New Zealand, was bullied in late January 2018 on an app called Sarahah that allows users to post anonymous messages. Among the hateful messages was one that said she should die.

Every year, the news is filled with reports like these of bullying incidents that happen in communities across the United States and the world. They underscore the need for antibullying measures that protect teens before anything happens and after an incident.

Social media apps can be a great way to connect but can also lead to cyberbullying. If an embarrassing video is posted on an app like Snapchat, it can cause the bullied student great distress

The Affected Parties

Bullying involves and affects three parties: victims, bystanders, and bullies. Teens with disabilities who experience any form of bullying are victims.

According to DoSomething.org, 3.2 million students in the United States are bullied each year. And 17 percent experience bullying multiple times a month or semester.

Despite these statistics, students do not always talk about the issue. DoSomething.org noted that by the time boys and girls are fourteen years old, only 30 percent of boys and 40 percent of girls will talk to other students about their traumatic encounters.

Why would a victim keep quiet? Fear of retribution is a main reason. Sometimes teens are simply embarrassed. They are ashamed that they could not avoid the situation or defend themselves. Perhaps that is why many teens do not even talk about bullying with their friends.

Bystanders are the second group impacted. These are classmates who witness an incident. A bully slams a victim into a locker, scattering his books everywhere. Some kids see trouble and flee. Others watch as if they're viewing entertainment. They don't take part but don't run for help either. Seeing a peer being hit, mocked, or otherwise harassed can be traumatic for bystanders. Over the next few days or weeks, some may also suffer anxiety, worrying if they're next. On the other hand, those who do nothing to assist a bullied teen may also suffer from guilt or other negative emotions.

While some bullies do not feel regret or remorse about their actions, generally, all bullies are at increased risk for emotional problems and substance abuse. They also can have lower grades and higher incidences of criminal behavior, such as stealing and vandalism, than other students. Bullies also face consequences for hurting peers, such as being expelled or suspended from school or being charged with a crime and going to jail.

How It Happens

Arguments and personality conflicts between teens are normal and are not considered bullying. Knowing how bullying does happen can help teens with disabilities figure out if they have been—or currently are—victims of bullying and prepare to safely address the issue.

Remember, bullying is usually defined as repeated behavior. Broad categories of bullying include physical, verbal, psychological, social, cyberbullying, and hazing.

Physical. A teen with disabilities subject to physical bullying may be hit, kicked, pushed, tripped, or otherwise physically harmed. Students bully teens with disabilities because they believe they may not be able to defend themselves. Being a victim of physical bullying may cause further harm to an area of the body already affected by a disability.

Verbal. Bullies use profanity, slurs, sarcasm, and name-calling to hurt their victims. They'll taunt teens with low vision about their eyesight, the way they hold books or tablets while reading, or where they sit in the classroom to see the blackboard. Some bullies also spread rumors at school, in the neighborhood, or online to expose teens to ridicule or embarrassment.

All teens want to have friends and feel like they belong, but students with disabilities may be particularly sensitive to being excluded from daily conversations and activities.

Psychological. Teens with disabilities can be subject to intimidation, harassment, and other behavior designed to impact their psychological well-being. Stalking also falls into this category. Stalking is a crime that occurs when a bully purposefully and repeatedly harasses someone. The bully may follow a person around nonstop and approach and physically attack the victim or stay at a distance making threatening gestures. Bullies also stalk by making threatening telephone calls or harassing victims on social media or social networks.

Social. Social bullying is designed to isolate teens with disabilities from other students, friends, and teammates by spreading rumors about them, excluding them from activities, or making fun of them in public. This type of bullying is more common with girls, but boys also use it to snub students or force them into situations where they are alone—or feel that way.

Cyberbullying. When teens use computers, cell phones, tablets, or other electronic equipment to harass or harm other students, it is considered cyberbullying. This type of bullying includes texts,

✋ Identity Revealed

Bullies adopt different strategies for hiding their true identity while engaging in cyberbullying. Some use fictitious names in chat rooms, on social media, and in messaging apps. Others try hiding their identities by using supposedly anonymous texting apps.

But there are ways to discover a bully's name, address, and other identifying information. Sometimes an account will have a debit or credit account attached to it, making it easy to determine who the bully is. In other cases, a computer used in cyberbullying can be traced to a person or home.

Bullied teens can take comfort in knowing that school and law enforcement personnel will work to reveal a cyberbully's true identity and impose disciplinary actions. Make sure to report all bullying so you can continue to enjoy spending time online.

Although social media can be a great way for teens with disabilities to connect, they must use caution online and be alert for any sign of cyberbullying, which must be reported.

emails, and offensive messages and photos posted on social media or in messaging apps.

Hazing. Hazing is humiliating treatment usually associated with joining a group, including sports teams and fraternities and sororities. It often includes one or more types of bullying, such as physical or verbal abuse, or being forced to engage in harmful activities, such as drinking large amounts of alcohol. Victims accept the hazing because they want to be a group member and believe they do not have a choice. This is not true. Many schools have developed antihazing programs, making it easier for teens, with or without disabilities, to report and stop this form of bullying.

All bullying is harmful—and scary. It not only places teens at risk of harm related to the specific type, but it also disturbs the emotional, mental, or psychological well-being of teens with disabilities.

Chapter Four

In Harm's Way

The Centers for Disease Control and Prevention (CDC) considers bullying a public health problem, categorizing it as a form of youth violence. According to the CDC's 2016 fact sheet "Understanding Bullying," in 2015, 20 percent of students reported being bullied at school. A slightly lower number—16 percent—said they experienced electronic bullying.

A Big Impact

Bullying affects both bullies and their victims. Teens with disabilities who are bullied may face emotional, social, or psychological harm. They may struggle with self-esteem and self-confidence issues. They also may have ongoing bouts of depression, anxiety, or health-related issues such as stomachaches and headaches. For teens with mental or emotional disabilities, these effects may be especially hard to cope with.

Bullies also cause physical injuries. Violent bullying can cause painful bruises, cuts, or wounds that require medical care, including hospitalization.

Tricking a teen with a food allergy into consuming the food that harms him is a form of bullying. When a teen in Pennsylvania with a severe pineapple allergy was unwittingly exposed to the fruit, she had to go to the hospital for treatment.

There are other forms of bullying that are more catastrophic, or even life threatening. Teens with food allergies may suffer life-threatening harm from bullying by other students who don't believe their issues are real.

That's what happened in December 2017 in Butler, Pennsylvania, when three middle school girls targeted another female student known to have a severe pineapple allergy. Their middle school cafeteria did not serve pineapple at that teen's lunch hour to protect the teen with the allergy. Despite that fact, the teens conspired to harm her.

A fruit cup was brought into the school. Then, while at lunch, one of the bullies slathered some pineapple juice on her hand then high-fived the unsuspecting victim, who immediately had a severe allergic reaction. Although she did not go into anaphylactic shock, according to a *Washington Post* article, she did require medical care at a hospital. Weeks after the incident, the bullies were charged with various crimes related to the incident.

For teens who bully, the goal is to gain power over their victims. The plan may backfire, however, if the bully starts to feel shame or guilt over what she did. She may also get in trouble at school or with law enforcement, which can lead to being expelled or worse.

"Bully-victims" is the term the CDC uses for students who bully other youth and also have been victims of bullying. Bully-victims are at risk of suffering more mental health and behavioral problems than students who fall into just one category as a bully or victim. They may have trouble forming friendships, exhibit signs of hyperactivity, and be more aggressive.

Empowered Bystander

Witnessing an act of bullying can be traumatic for nonvictims, also known as bystanders. Some may be afraid for their own safety and flee the scene, without notifying anyone of the incident. Doing so limits a school administrator's ability to respond quickly to the situation.

Other bystanders may simply watch or even join in on the bullying. A third set of bystanders try to diffuse the situation or seek out immediate assistance. These students are called upstanders.

Upstanders make schools better by striving to do what is right. They speak up against bullying attacks, help a friend get out of harm's

(continued on the next page)

(continued from the previous page)

way, and make sure administrators know about any bullying behavior.

Upstanders model inclusion, respect, and acceptance by associating with students from many different backgrounds and encouraging peers to do the same. Upstanders reach out a hand to students who might feel isolated, making an effort to eat with them or include them in activities. Every school and community needs upstanders, and teens with disabilities can become informed, engaged participants who help thwart bullying.

Responses to Bullying

Teens with disabilities can react to bullying in both constructive or destructive ways. Of course, the more constructive the response the better it is for the victim and those around him, but destructive responses include the following:

Denial. Teens with disabilities may deny they are being bullied because they fear retribution or because they do not want to draw increased attention to themselves or their disabilities. Denial won't stop bullying. Victims must first acknowledge the abuse before working to combat the bullying.

Self-blame. Many teens blame themselves for another teen's cruelty, but victims are never at fault. Teens with disabilities who blame themselves for being bullied should seek professional help to overcome the feelings of shame and self-blame.

Social isolation. After being bullied, some teens with disabilities distance themselves from classmates and have few friends because they do not know whom they can trust. But isolating oneself may lead to increased bullying, as bullies target loners. Consider joining the chorus, literary magazine, or other club to meet people who can offer friendship and support.

Truancy. According to DoSomething.org, about 160,000 teens don't go to school each day due to bullying. And worse, one in ten students who are repeatedly bullied drop out of school altogether. Don't let abuse highjack your educational goals. Learn prevention strategies to beat bullying so that skipping or quitting school are not options.

Self-harm. Harming oneself by cutting or other methods is a destructive response to a bullying event. Feelings of despair can even lead a teen to contemplate suicide. Teens have completed suicide and left notes or video messages attributing bullying as the reason for their suicidal actions. If you are feeling suicidal, get immediate help. The Suicide Hotline (800-273-8255) is open twenty-four hours a day, seven days a week.

Retaliation. Bully-victims are teens who have experienced both sides of the bullying issue. They have been targets of mean acts and have bullied other teens. It is difficult to imagine wanting someone else to feel the hurt, shame,

When teens internalize bullying or don't seek help, they are more likely to feel depressed and hopeless. Some teens who feel this way may end up engaging in self-harm. The National Suicide Prevention Hotline (800-273-8255) offers confidential help twenty-four hours a day, seven days a week.

or despair associated with bullying. However, retaliating against innocent people is a frequent response to many types of trauma, including bullying. Don't retaliate; get even with bullies by reporting actions so they can face consequences for their behavior.

On April 20, 1999, two students at Columbine High School in Littleton, Colorado, killed twelve students and one teacher while injuring more than twenty other students. The perpetrators, Eric Harris and Dylan Klebold, are said to have been bullied. Some thought they hurt others as punishment for the hurt they endured. Other school shootings and violent acts at schools since have likely been conducted by other bully-victims.

According to the *Spokesman-Review*, on September 13, 2017, Caleb Sharpe killed one student and injured others at Freeman High School in Spokane, Washington, for allegedly being bullied by the boy he killed. Reportedly, he had watched documentaries about other school shootings, including the one at Columbine High School.

Hurting others is never an effective answer to the pain, frustration, or anger teens feel as bullying victims. Seek help from a trusted adult if you feel out of control and alone.

✋ Food for Thought

Teens with disabilities may have conditions that other students have trouble understanding because the disabilities are invisible, such as chronic pain, mental illness, or autism. Allergic reactions are another form of invisible disability. These allergies can be serious and debilitating. Allergies to nuts, pollen, and bees are well-known medical conditions. However, an allergy to a specific food (such as pineapple) or fabric (such as latex used in rubber gloves) may be less familiar to most teens. Not knowing about a condition is never a reason to mock, isolate, or endanger someone. And exposing a person to an allergen as a prank puts that person's life at risk and may end in the bully facing criminal charges.

Constructive Responses

It's vital for teens with disabilities who have been bullied to acknowledge that they are being victimized. Once they accept this fact, they can address the issue in ways that are constructive for everyone involved.

If you're being bullied, you can talk about your disability with your peers. While it's not your job to educate others, working to dispel any ignorance or superstitions surrounding disability can result in

True friends will accept you no matter your disability. But educating others about your condition may help lessen the stigma around disability and perhaps lead to less bullying.

positive change. It's easier for a bully to lash out at something he or she doesn't understand, so try to bridge that gap—but only in ways that feel safe for you.

Using a classroom assignment, such as a report or essay, to enlighten peers about a disability may help other teens understand the condition and perhaps prevent some bullying.

Bullies prey on people with low self-esteem. If a teen feels insecure, uncomfortable, or embarrassed because of a difference, he may be seen as a potential victim. Becoming comfortable with your disability may boost self-esteem and confidence and make you less of a target for bullies.

Accepting your disability helps give you the confidence to face the future with the enthusiasm and energy needed to achieve your desired goals. This acceptance also fosters self-love and potentially hinders self-harming tendencies.

Another effective response to bullying is reporting incidences. Victims can't get help if educators, school administrators, safety personnel, or other trusted adults are unaware that bullying is happening. By speaking up, you are working to make your school safer for everyone.

10 Great Questions to Ask a Victim's Advocate

1. How does your agency help teens with disabilities who are bullied?

2. How important is an advocate in helping teens beat bullying?

3. What should teens know about working with an advocate?

4. Have you ever been bullied yourself?

5. Can an advocate help a bullied teen talk with a parent or guardian about the problem?

6. Is it possible to feel safe again once you've been bullied?

7. How can a teen with a disability overcome the self-blame game after being bullied?

8. Is staying off the internet the only protection against cyberbullying?

9. What can teens do to help friends who are bullying other students because they were once victims?

10. How can I join with others to fight bullying?

Chapter Five

Beating Bullying

There is an epidemic of bullying in this country, which has brought about a greater commitment to addressing the issue. The federal government, states and cities, school systems, organizations, and individuals are working toward the goal of keeping students safe at school and other places where they gather.

Students with disabilities face bullying at a higher rate than their nondisabled peers. Despite the frequency of incidences, these teens can beat bullying. To do so, they need to use strategies that have been proven effective and find healthy ways to deal with the stress that comes from being bullied.

Exercising Rights

Teens with disabilities have rights under existing laws and under their school's bullying prevention policies. The 1990 Americans with Disabilities Act (ADA) is a civil rights law that protects teens against discrimination based on a disability. The 1975 Individuals with Disabilities Education Act (IDEA) affected how students were taught and the services they received in school.

IDEA was enacted to give students with disabilities access to special education and services that met their needs. It required that affected students receive a "free appropriate public education" (FAPE). It made it mandatory that schools provide safe environments where students can learn without restrictions.

To assure students receive an education in a restriction-free environment, schools develop Individualized Education Programs (IEPs) for students with special needs. Hearing, vision, and speech impairments, learning disabilities, and brain injuries are among the disabilities that qualify a student to have an IEP. An IEP outlines a specific plan for educating a student. It includes his or her learning needs, related services to accommodate any disability, and ways to measure progress.

Experts at PACER's National Bullying Prevention Center (www.pacer .org) suggest that IEPs can be used to define how incidents of bullying are reported and documented by school staff. IEPs can also be used to make sure that students have school staff who shadow them. Shadowing is a procedure that allows staff to follow students at designated times throughout the day, keeping them safe.

At IEP meetings, such as the one shown here, the educational team can determine how to best protect the student with a disability from bullying, as well as how to report any bullying incidents that do occur.

In addition to their rights under the ADA, students with disabilities have rights under the school's antibullying rules and codes of conduct. Students with disabilities should become familiar with these rules and codes in order to help combat bullying.

Teens with disabilities can also learn about school-related antibullying laws. Although there is no federal antibullying law, there are state laws. In 1999, Georgia enacted the first such law after an Atlanta teen was brutally beaten at a school bus stop. Today, laws exist in all fifty states and the District of Columbia.

Many states have also included cyberbullying in antibullying laws. One area that has received increased attention in recent years is dating-related cyberbullying attacks. These include when someone posts nude or other private pictures in order to publicly shame a person he or she has dated. Such behavior has exposed victims to increased bullying, as well as hostility and ridicule from other teens, whether at their own school or from the far corners of the internet. In rare instances, some victims have died by suicide after feeling the deep shame associated with having their private lives exposed.

Focusing on Safety First

When confronting a bully, always put safety first. If a bullying incident escalates to the point where you feel unsafe, you should remove yourself from the situation as quickly as possible. Which safety-first strategies work well?

- Getting away. Avoid being cornered in a place where there are no teachers or students who could help.
- Responding briefly. In some instances, it may be appropriate to respond to a bully's hateful words by saying something like "Don't talk to me that way" or "That's not true. Stop it."
- Releasing emotions. In *Odd Girl Out*, Rachel Simmons suggests, "Get a diary or journal and write about your feelings. Paint, dance, kick-box, run in the rain, punch a bag, write a song, bang on drums. Don't keep it inside. The way to fight back is to release."
- Keeping personal things confidential. Guard all personal information—including photos and texts—and don't give bullies material to use against you.

It is also a good idea to evaluate your social media presence. In her book *The Survival Guide to Bullying Written by a Teen*, Aija Mayrock shares her experience with cyberbullying. She suggests teens "go dark"—take a complete break from social media—to fight cyberbullying. Going "almost dark" is a strategy she suggests to help teens minimize online interactions by engaging on only one or two preferred social platforms.

Celebrating Differences and Speaking Up

When a teen with a disability dislikes himself because he is physically different or processes information differently he is at extra risk of being socially isolated and more vulnerable. Conversely, when a teen celebrates her differences, she is better able to keep a positive outlook on life, make friends, and reduce vulnerability based on low self-esteem or low self-confidence.

It is also vital to speak up about bullying, which many students seem reluctant to do. They may be embarrassed and feel like they should be able to handle the situation on their own. Or they may fear that the bully will step up his attacks if his actions are exposed.

Rehearsing a conversation may also be useful. It may seem odd, but as Rachel Simmons notes in *Odd Girl Out*, "adults rehearse difficult conversations all the time, with good reason: just as practicing piano or soccer makes you a better player, practicing how you communicate makes you more effective in your relationships."

It takes courage to talk about bullying but speaking up can lead to getting help from parents, educators, school administrators, and peers. A teen's support system can't help him beat bullying if they aren't given accurate, complete information. In some cases, teens may have to seek medical help or professional counseling for assistance with anxiety, fear, sleep disorders, or other problems that stem from being bullied.

Examining Friendships

Every teen needs true friends who are trustworthy, reliable, and supportive. Unfortunately, as many teens discover, some peers don't live up to those expectations. Sometimes a so-called friend is also

✋ On the Calendar

October is National Bullying Prevention Month. Participating in related events offers students a chance to talk and learn more about beating bullying. The month-long campaign is spearheaded by PACER'S National Bullying Prevention Center, and there are many different ways to get involved. For example, students can join in social media campaigns to spread the word about antibullying. They can sign a digital "Together Against Bullying" pledge, attend programs at their school at which students or guest speakers share their stories, or host an event within the larger community to spread awareness and offer solutions to the problem of bullying. PACER offers sample agendas and other information to make events successful on its website.

During National Bullying Prevention Month, teens can get involved in activities that bring awareness to the issue, encourage advocacy, and show support for victims of bullying.

the bully who hurts, taunts, or is otherwise mean to a teen with a disability. Or they act like friends when alone but like enemies around other students.

Friends turning into frenemies is probably one of the most agonizing aspects of bullying. Teens with disabilities must ask themselves whether staying friends with a person like this is worth the trauma and upset. The answer is usually a resounding no—especially if that friend has been given an opportunity to change but refuses to do so.

Odd Girl Out author Rachel Simmons suggests that parents ask their children the following questions about friendships:

- "What are you looking for in a good friend?
- Does this person give you that?
- Why do you think you are staying friends with someone who makes you feel this way?"

Regularly examining friendships helps teens determine which friends are positive influences on their lives. After cutting ties with the toxic people in their lives, teens can develop new and healthier friendships. It is not always easy to make friends, but there are other students looking for authentic connections, too. When teens actively seek out new relationships, they can find like-minded peers in classes, clubs, after-school activities, and at part-time jobs.

Getting Involved

There are several ways teens with disabilities can help beat bullying. To begin with, they can offer support

🖐 Libraries Fight Against Bullying

Teens with disabilities concerned about bullying at school and in the community have an ally in libraries and their staff. Library personnel are providing antibullying information, programs, and other resources to bring awareness and to keep libraries bully-free zones.

According to Beverly Goldberg, writing in *American Libraries* magazine, the American Association of School Libraries found that 70 percent of responding librarians had addressed bullying in some way. They have helped answer questions, share information on safe internet use, and participated in antibullying community programs.

April Lesher, a junior high school librarian in Mesa, Arizona, started a program called the Friendship Project. According to Anne Ford, writing in *American Libraries* magazine, the Friendship Project is "a multifaceted program designed to give students a safe, fun place to learn from and connect with one another" by helping "students make friends, acquire new abilities, practice leadership skills, and feel more confident."

to other victims. The Substance Abuse and Mental Health Services Administration (SAMHSA) fact sheet "Stop Bullying: Be More Than A Bystander" notes that students can help other students know they are not alone by "discouraging the bully, defending the victim, or redirecting the situation away from bullying." A teen can also help other victims by reporting bullying, especially if a friend is reluctant to do so. Reports can be given openly or anonymously.

Teens can get involved in activities or organizations that help them maximize their potential or showcase their unique talents. Science and math competitions and spelling bees help students with disabilities compete against teens with and without disabilities. Meanwhile, participating in Special Olympics events, for example, lets students compete against other athletes with disabilities. All of these events affirm students' skills, while proving that students with disabilities can succeed in any arena.

By showcasing their unique talents, students with disabilities, like these cheerleaders at the Special Olympics, build self-confidence, and fight against the stereotype of what it means to have a disability.

Another way to help is to become an antibullying advocate. Teens can join school and community organizations focused on prevention. They can give their gifts and talents to those groups working to keep teens safe every day. Or students with disabilities can start efforts at their schools. While still a high school student in Rhode Island, Brandon Greene came up with an idea to develop a school project focused on antibullying. Its focus was helping improve the school atmosphere and inspiring students to be active bystanders. The program became a school-wide success and expanded its focus to include coat drives and other community service projects. At the 2011 White House Conference on Bullying Prevention, President Barack Obama acknowledged Brandon's advocacy.

The Long Term

In an ideal world, teens with disabilities would not have to endure bullying's physical, emotional, and psychological abuse. Unfortunately, teens have never lived in an ideal world. Bullying is prevalent, and nothing indicates that the problem will go away anytime soon. Instead, the rise of social media has led to cyberbullying, adding another layer of torment to those already feeling under attack.

Teens with disabilities may think that bullying stops in high school. It does not. Mean teens go to college and continue targeting students who have no idea of their attacker's history of bullying. In addition, bullies who do not go to college take jobs at local places, where teens with disabilities might spend a lot of time. That's the bad news.

The good news is that once teens learn effective skills for beating bullies, they can use those for the rest of their lives. Teens with disabilities can head to college confident that they have antibullying tools that work, including how to find useful resources at their new school. From their experiences in high school, they now know they can look for college

Never give up hope! It's possible to beat bullying, lead a happy, productive life, and make lasting friendships at school and in your community.

organizations for students with disabilities, seek out advisors and other staff for help navigating structural or technological access, and join antibullying efforts on campus. Or teens with disabilities can take jobs in the community following high school and know that their successful antibullying strategies work as well in the workplace as they do in high school.

Courage and tenacity are required to beat bullying. Hope also is essential. If teens with disabilities believe nothing will ever change, they will not resist bullying. Keep a positive, winning attitude. Don't give up on enjoying a life free from cruel behavior from other students.

Also resist the temptation to hurt peers. Becoming the aggressor is not the right way to beat bullying. Choosing to be kind to other teens while accepting them and their disabilities is the right approach.

Teens with disabilities seeking to make positive impacts on their schools and communities can begin exploring ways to beat bullying today. Involved teens empower themselves and their peers while creating bully-free zones everywhere teens gather, including at school.

Glossary

allergen Something that causes an allergic reaction.

amputee A person who has had a body part, such as an arm or leg, surgically removed.

anaphylactic shock A life-threatening medical condition caused by an allergic reaction, which can adversely affect breathing and lead to death in extreme cases.

autism A developmental disability affecting a person's behavior, communication, and social interactions.

bipolar disorder A medical term for a specific diagnosed mental illness usually adversely affecting a person's moods and behavior and involving periods of depression and mania.

Centers for Disease Control and Prevention (CDC) The federal health protection agency in the United States; it protects Americans against, and responds to, health threats.

chronic pain Persistent pain lasting more than three months and caused by varying factors, including disability or injury.

conspire To unite for purposes of devising an evil plot or scheme.

Crohn's disease A disease of the digestive track resulting in chronic inflammation.

dwarfism Unusually low stature or small size often caused by genetics.

dyslexia A learning disability that is makes it difficult for a person to read, spell, or write.

obsessive-compulsive disorder (OCD) A type

of mental health disorder related to anxiety and seen in a person's repeated, persistent thoughts and behavior.

paraplegia A condition in which a person has limited or no ability to move lower parts of her body.

perpetrator A person who commits an injustice or crime.

Tourette's syndrome A chronic disorder of the nervous system evidenced by involuntary movements or sounds.

whiplash An injury occurring to the neck from trauma such as a car accident or other violent incident.

For More Information

Beyond Bullies
(424) 253-6702
Website: http://www.beyondbullies.org
Facebook and Twitter: @BeyondBullies
Instagram: beyond_bullies
Beyond Bullies provides extensive antibullying resources, including videos, social media campaigns and related hashtags, online antibullying training, and a form for site visitors to share their stories. Resources are also available in Spanish.

BullyBust
National School Climate Center
341 West 38th Street, 9th floor
New York, NY 10018
(212) 707-8799
Website: https://bullybust.org/students
Facebook: @upstander
Twitter: @bullybust
YouTube: @schoolclimate
BullyBust helps students and adults get involved in bullying prevention. Available materials include general topical information, victim stories, a "Stand Up Pledge," and links to organizations that offer students help or information.

Bullying Canada Inc.
471 Smythe Street
PO Box 27009
Fredericton, NB E3B 9M1
Canada

(800) 352-4497
Website: https://www.bullyingcanada.ca
Bullying Canada focuses on providing resources
    for all parties affected by bullying and offers
    a national hotline, speakers' program, and
    other resources.

The Bully Project
18 W. 27th Street
2nd Floor
New York, NY 10001
(212) 725-1220
Website: https://www.thebullyproject.com
Facebook, Twitter, and Instagram: @bullymovie
The Bully Project is put together by the creators of
    Bully the film, and offers resources to prevent
    bullying, including a confidential hotline in con-
    junction with its partner, 121Help.Me.

PACER's Teens Against Bullying
8161 Normandale Boulevard
Minneapolis, MN 55437
(952) 838-9000
Website: https://www.pacerteensagainstbullying.org
Facebook: @PACERsNationalBullyingPreventionCenter
Instagram: @pacer_nbpc
Developed by the PACER National Bullying Preven-
    tion Center, the teen-focused site provides tools
    to beat bullying, such as videos, stories, quizzes,
    and a student action plan.

Promoting Relationships and Preventing Violence
    Network (PREVNet)

PREVNet
Queens University
90 Barrie Street
Kingston, ON K7L 3N5
Canada
(613) 533-2632; 800-372-2495
Kids Help Phone: (800) 668-6868
Website: https://www.prevnet.ca
Facebook, Twitter, and Instagram: @PREVNet
YouTube: PREVNet Coordin
PREVNet is a network of scientists and organiza-
    tions dedicated to stopping bullying in Canada.
    Resources include pages for both bullies and vic-
    tims, videos, and a helpline.

Stopbullying.gov
US Department of Health and Human Services
200 Independence Avenue SW
Washington, DC 20201
Website: https://www.stopbullying.gov
Facebook: @Stopbullying.gov
Twitter: @StopBullyingGov
YouTube: @StopbullyingGov
Instagram: @stopbullyinggov
StopBullying.gov is a federal government website
    containing information from various agencies
    about bullying and cyberbullying. It includes a
    page for teens that discusses what they can do
    to beat bullying.

For Further Reading

Adams, Serena. *Everything You Need to Know About Trolls and Cybermobs* (Need to Know Library). New York, NY: Rosen Publishing, 2017.

Brezina, Corona. *Helping a Friend Who Is Being Bullied (How Can I Help? Friends Helping Friends)*. New York, NY: Rosen Publishing, 2017.

Brezina, Corona. *Standing Up to Bullying at School (The LGBTQ+ Guide to Beating Bullying)*. New York, NY: Rosen Publishing, 2017.

Burcaw, Shane. *Laughing at My Nightmare.* New York, NY: Square Fish, 2016.

Criswell, Patti Kelley. *Stand Up for Yourself & Your Friends: Dealing with Bullies & Bossiness and Finding a Better Way.* Middleton, WI: American Girl, 2016.

Donahue, Mary P. *Surviving Bullies and Mean Teens (Teen Survival Guide)*. New York, NY: Enslow Publishing, 2018.

Haugen, David, Susan Musser, and Michael Chaney, eds. *Teens Rights and Freedoms: Bullying.* Farmington Hills, MI: Greenhaven Press, 2014.

Landau, Jennifer, ed. *Teens Talk About Learning Disabilities and Differences (Teen Voices: Real Teens Discuss Real Problems)*. New York, NY: Rosen Publishing, 2018.

Maciel, Amanda. *Tease.* New York, NY: Balzer + Bray, 2015.

Mayrock, Aija. *The Survival Guide to Bullying Written by a Teen.* New York, NY: Scholastic, Inc., 2015.

Bibliography

Bully Project, The. "Bullying and the Law: A Guide for Parents." Retrieved January 5, 2018. http://www.thebullyproject.com/bullying_the_law.

Criswell, Patti Kelley, *Stand Up for Yourself & Your Friends.* Middleton, WI: American Girl, 2016.

DoSomething.org. "11 Facts About Bullying." Retrieved December 30, 2017. https://www.dosomething.org/us/facts/11-facts-about-bullying.

Goldberg, Beverly. "How Libraries Help Kids Stand Up to Bullying." *American Libraries*, October 1, 2014.https://americanlibrariesmagazine.org/2014/10/01/how-libraries-help-kids-stand-up-to-bullying.

Haugen, David, Susan Musser, and Michael Chaney, eds. *Teens Rights and Freedoms: Bullying.* Farmington Hills, MI: Greenhaven Press, 2014.

Holsman, Jessica. *The High School Survival Guide: Your Guide to Studying, Socializing, and Succeeding.* Miami, FL: Mango, 2016.

Landau, Jennifer. *The Middle School Survival Handbook: Dealing with Bullies, Cliques, and Social Stress.* New York, NY: Rosen Publishing, 2013.

Lerner, Janet, and Beverly Johns. *Learning Disabilities and Related Disabilities: Strategies for Success.* Belmont, CA: Wadsworth Publishing, 2014.

Lohmann, Raychelle Cassada, and Julia V. Taylor. *The Bullying Workbook for Teens*. Oakland, CA: Instant Help Books, 2013.

Miller, Cindy, and Cynthia Lowen. *The Essential Guide to Bullying Prevention and Intervention.*

New York, NY: Alpha Books, 2012.

Musgrove, Melody, and Michael K. Yudin. "Dear Colleague Letter on Bullying." U.S. Department of Education, Office of Special Education and Rehabilitative Services, August 20, 2013. https://www2.ed.gov/policy/speced/guid/idea/memosdcltrs/bullyingdcl-8-20-13.pdf.

National Center for Injury Prevention and Control, Division of Violence Prevention, Centers for Disease Control and Prevention. "Understanding Bullying Fact Sheet 2016." Retrieved February 5, 2018.https://www.cdc.gov/violenceprevention/pdf/bullying_factsheet.pdf.

Nuwer, Hank. *Hazing: Destroying Young Lives.* Bloomington, IN: Indiana University Press, 2018.

Pacer's National Bullying Prevention Center. "The Individualized Education Program (IEP) and Bullying." Retrieved January 15, 2018. http://www.pacer.org/publications/bullypdf/BP-4.pdf.

Rose, Chad A., and Nicholas A. Gage. Exceptional Children. "Exploring the Involvement of Bullying Among Students with Disabilities Over Time." Retrieved January 27, 2017. http://journals.sagepub.com.

Sokol, Leslie, and Marci G. Fox. *Think Confident, Be Confident, Workbook for Teens: Activities to Help You Create Unshakable Self-Confidence and Reach Your Goals.* Oakland, CA: New Harbinger Publications, 2016.

StopBullying.gov. "Cyberbullying Tactics." Retrieved January 29, 2018. https://www.stopbullying.gov/cyberbullying/cyberbullying-tactics/index.html.

StopBullying.gov. "Warning Signs of Bullying."

Retrieved January 15, 2018. https://
www.stopbullying.gov/at-risk/warning-signs
/index.html.

StopBullying.gov. "What Is Cyberbullying."
Retrieved January 15, 2018. https://
www.stopbullying.gov/cyberbullying/what-is-it
/index.html.

Yudin, Michael. "Keeping Students with Disabilities
Safe from Bullying." Homeroom Blog, August 23,
2013. https://blog.ed.gov/2013/08/keeping
-students-with-disabilities-safe-from-bullying.

Index

About the Author

Born with a physical difference of just two fingers on her left hand, Lisa A. Crayton knows what it is like to be bullied as a teen and how to safely overcome the social problem. A former corporate publications editor and writer, she loves writing for children and teens. She is the author or coauthor of numerous other books for youth. She loves mentoring writers and especially enjoys speaking at writers' conferences. She earned a master of fine arts degree from National University and a bachelor's degree in public relations and journalism, cum laude, from Utica College.

Photo Credits